O CANADA
TED HARRISON

TICKNOR & FIELDS

New York

1993

First American edition 1993 published by Ticknor & Fields,
A Houghton Mifflin company, 215 Park Avenue South,
New York, New York 10003.

First published in Canada by Kids Can Press Ltd.

Manufactured in the United States of America
Text of this book is set in 14 pt. Goudy Oldstyle.
The illustrations are acrylic paintings, reproduced in full color.

HOR   10 9 8 7 6 5 4 3 2 1

Library of Congress Cataloging-in-Publication Data

Harrison, Ted, 1926-
    O Canada / Ted Harrison. — 1st American ed.
        p.   cm.
    Summary: Includes the author's paintings and brief descriptions of
the various provinces and territories in Canada.
    ISBN 0-395-66075-0
    1. Canada—Juvenile literature. [1. Canada—Description and
travel.]   I. Title.
    F1008.2.H33   1993
    971—dc20   92-39800   CIP   AC

INTRODUCTION

Canada and the United States share the longest undefended border in the world. We are each other's biggest trading partners. We have in common TV shows, movies, books, and music. But we are also quite different. It is a tribute to both nations that we get along so well.

Canada is a democracy, but unlike the United States, we have a prime minister rather than a president. Our formal head of state is a governor-general who represents Canada's monarch, Queen Elizabeth II. We have two official languages—English and French—and the country is divided into provinces and territories rather than states.

Canada's history is also different from U.S. history. Our lands are home to some of the same indigenous populations, and we have had similar patterns of immigration. But we established independence from Britain peacefully in 1867, when a collection of British colonies came together to form a Dominion. Our connection to Britain has remained strong, and our government is based on that country's model, as are our laws and many of our customs.

People may think of Canadians as being "quieter" than Americans. For one thing, there are not nearly so many of us. Although in terms of area, Canada is the second biggest country in the world, only 27 million people inhabit it. That's slightly fewer than the number of people living in the state of California. For another, we are not in the habit of speaking out about our country and our love for it in the same way Americans do. But we are a proud nation. We think Canada is a good place to live.

I was not born in Canada but I came here more than twenty-five years ago and I have since become a citizen. In a tribute to my adopted country, I have painted my vision of every province and territory. I invite my American friends to get to know this beautiful land to the north. The illustrations show Canada as I see it. To me it is a land of color and wonder.

Bon voyage.

TED HARRISON
Whitehorse, Yukon Territory

ARCTIC OCEAN

BEAUFORT
SEA

ALASKA

VICTORIA
ISLAND

• Dawson
YUKON
TERRITORY

Great Bear Lake

NORTHWEST TERRITORIES

ALASKAN PANHANDLE

• Whitehorse

• Yellowknife

Great Slave Lake

BRITISH
COLUMBIA

ALBERTA

SASKATCHEWAN

MANIT

QUEEN CHARLOTTE
ISLANDS

• Edmonton

Flin Flon

*Lake
Winnipeg*

VANCOUVER ISLAND

• Calgary

Victoria •

• Vancouver

Regina •

Winnipeg

PACIFIC

OCEAN

UNITED STATES

CANADA

(Not to scale)

• Alert

ELLESMERE ISLAND

ATLANTIC

OCEAN

BAFFIN ISLAND

HUDSON

BAY

NEWFOUNDLAND
AND LABRADOR

Churchill

LABRADOR

ISLAND OF
NEWFOUNDLAND

OBA

QUEBEC

ONTARIO

PRINCE EDWARD
ISLAND

NOVA SCOTIA

Quebec •

Halifax •

Lake Superior

Montreal •

Lake Huron

Ottawa ★

NEW BRUNSWICK

Toronto
•

Lake Michigan

Lake Ontario

Lake Erie

NEWFOUNDLAND AND LABRADOR

In this region, known simply as Newfoundland, the land is rocky and the winters are cold and windy. But it is very beautiful with its green flat-topped mountains and seaside fishing villages of brightly painted houses. The ocean is cold and clear; a peek over the edge of any wharf affords a view of the ocean floor, even where the green-blue water is deepest. There, fish swim and crabs scurry. In the spring, majestic icebergs float by. Some of them are as big as apartment buildings, although only one-seventh of their mass is visible above water. The rest is hidden below.

When I think of Newfoundland, I always think of the sea. For hundreds of years it teemed with lobster, cod, herring, and whales. It's been said that in the early days, the sea was so full of cod the fishermen could reach over the sides of their boats and grab the fish right out of the water with their hands. There are not nearly so many cod now, but limits on the number that can be fished in the next few years will help the supply replenish itself.

Newfoundland, the easternmost point of Canada, is an island in the Atlantic Ocean, and Labrador is on the mainland, stretching in a triangular strip along the Labrador Sea. Newfoundlanders have always depended on the sea for their living and for communication. Until recently, there were no roads between villages and everything came by boat: groceries, mail, even family and friends. Maybe that is what makes them so generous and welcoming. No one is ever treated as a stranger.

NOVA SCOTIA

Nova Scotia has modern towns and a bustling capital city, Halifax, but that is not what I think of when someone mentions this province by name. To me, it is a grand procession of meandering roads and picturesque villages full of wonderful old houses. It is almost entirely surrounded by water and is connected to the rest of Canada only by a narrow strip of land. Nowhere in the province is the sea more than forty miles away. Almost everyone lives in seaside communities, which are connected by the twisting, turning roads that follow the coast.

This province has been settled for a long time and although there have always been farmers in the region, most Nova Scotians have made their living from the sea. In the early days, they worked as fishermen, shipbuilders, and sailors who traveled all over the world. The region has been a hiding place for pirates and privateers; one legend tells how the famous Captain Kidd buried his treasure on a small island there and never came back for it. When I drive past the harbors and bays and the villages with their olden-days houses, my thoughts are of all those stories and legends that the people remember as if they happened yesterday, and not hundreds of years ago.

PRINCE EDWARD ISLAND

Prince Edward Island is a land of endless white sand beaches and fertile brick-red soil. There are no big cities here, only pristine towns kept so clean they seem as if they have just been washed. Out in the countryside, farmhouses painted white sit beside rolling fields of potatoes that run right down to the sea.

The coastal waters of Prince Edward Island are full of reefs and sandbars that are dangerous to the fishermen and sailors. That is why there are so many lighthouses all around the island. For hundreds of years, keepers lit the lamps by hand each day at sundown. A ship that returned home after dark would be guided safely into the harbor by sailors who could see the flash of the warning light. Today all the lighthouses come on automatically, just as streetlights do, as important to the lives of seafaring folk as they ever were.

Islanders live a quiet life—and they like it that way. Their history is a proud one; it was here that the Fathers of Confederation met in 1864 and decided to make Canada a country. The island's residents do not like to change old ways too quickly. Friendships last a lifetime, just as they did in the time of *Anne of Green Gables*.

NEW BRUNSWICK

New Brunswick always surprises and delights me with its varied landscape. Fishing villages run along the coast, farmland along the Saint John River, and miles of forest cover the rest of the province. It has lovely old towns of English-speaking residents, whose ancestors left the United States after the War of Independence; and it has serene towns of French-speaking inhabitants, the Acadians, descendants of the original French settlers.

One coast of New Brunswick runs along the Bay of Fundy. The bay is so long and narrow that the force of the ocean creates tides fifty-two feet high, or as tall as a five-story building, that rush in as fast as a person can walk. The size and shape of the bay have made it a special place, with plants, seaweed, and creatures that are different from those found anywhere else in the world. At the mouth of the bay is Grand Manan Island, a bare but scenic place that is a safe haven for thousands of birds.

Up the Saint John River and into the heart of the province are farm fields, cows, and thoroughbred horses. Beyond that is the New Brunswick forest, which covers more than eighty-five percent of the province. It is one of the largest temperate forests left anywhere in the world.

QUEBEC

When I stand on a street corner in one of Quebec's cities, I am always aware of how different it is from the rest of Canada. The older streets have houses made of stone built right out to the sidewalk. Everyone around me is speaking French, and there is constant laughter and bustle. Quebec has the largest French-speaking population outside France. Its people have a culture unlike that found anywhere else in the country.

Many of the French came to Quebec first for the fur trade. They made friends with the Native people they met and adopted many of their ways and customs. Many traveled by river deep into the country and trapped and traded for furs to sell in France. They were known as the "coureurs de bois," the runners of the woods, and they were the first to discover much of the interior of North America. Later on, farmers settled the towns and the land, and villages grew up along the St. Lawrence River, but these first explorers left stories and legends as exciting as Daniel Boone's.

Eventually Quebec came under British control. But the original settlers did not give up their language or their culture, and 230 years later, French is still spoken in Quebec.

ONTARIO

More people live in Ontario than anywhere else in Canada—almost forty percent of the entire population. What always surprises me is that most of them inhabit the very small part of the province known as Southern Ontario. Canada's biggest city, Toronto, is a bustling, multicultural burg, where the sound of nearly every language in the world can be heard in the streets. As in any big city today almost anything a person desires is here. It could be a ticket to a game of the top-rated baseball team, the Toronto Blue Jays. It could be a visit to a museum or art gallery. Or it could be a day spent shopping in the city's many stores.

Millions of Canadians and Americans travel back and forth across the border every year for business and for fun. But in the War of 1812, we were not such good friends. The American fleet captured and set fire to the town of York, now called Toronto. In revenge, British and Canadian troops slipped into Washington and burned the presidential mansion (later known as the White House) and other government buildings. It is the only time the United States was successfully invaded and the last time the United States and Canada have been on opposite sides in a war.

Although I always like to visit Toronto, it's the countryside I like best. I love the pretty towns and the rolling farmland of southern Ontario. I also love the untouched wilderness of northern Ontario. It is so huge and so empty that many places do not even have roads. The only way to get in and out of some of those towns is by bush plane. That's an adventure!

MANITOBA

Southern Manitoba is mostly farmland. Endless fields of sunflowers and wheat make the province look as if it has been painted bright yellow in the summertime. Winnipeg, the capital city, is a main link between the eastern, western, and northern parts of Canada. It's a city of artists, home to a lively theater and music community, and to Canada's most famous dance company, the Royal Winnipeg Ballet.

Northern Manitoba is wilderness and mining country where the Native people can still pursue their traditional way of life—hunting, trapping, and fishing. In Flin Flon, one of the northern mining towns, it gets so cold in winter that the town's water pipes have been enclosed in long insulated wooden boxes built above ground. These would freeze if they were underground.

In Churchill, a town on the shores of Hudson Bay, people shop, go to the movies, and even go to school under one roof because of the winter cold. Its residents have to check the street carefully before going out in March in case there are polar bears wandering around. Every spring the bears leave the safety of the ice floes, which tend to drift toward Churchill, to find food. They've discovered that the town dump has many tasty tidbits and now make stopping there an annual event.

SASKATCHEWAN

Saskatchewan is prairie country where the grasslands have become Canada's greatest wheat-producing area. Here the skies seem endless because the land is so flat, and grain elevators are the abiding landmark of the province. In summer the golden grain stretches for miles before it meets the horizon of the usually cloudless blue sky.

The Royal Canadian Mounted Police, or the Mounties, have their training school in the capital city of Regina. They are Canada's national police force and they have a long, distinguished history. They were first known as the North West Mounted Police when they fanned out across the Canadian west in 1873 to maintain law and order in the new land; because of them, Canada did not have the "Wild West" experience of the United States. The settlers, ranchers, Native people, and gold-rush prospectors learned to respect the red-coated men on their well-trained horses.

Today, the Mounties are more likely to be found driving cars than riding horses, but they have not forgotten their past. They maintain a mounted unit; their very best horses and riders train for a long time to be able to perform the precision moves that have made their traveling show, known as the Musical Ride, famous.

ALBERTA

Alberta shares a vast prairie land with Saskatchewan. But soon the grasslands give way to the rolling foothills that lead to the peaks of the Rocky Mountains. This is Canada's modern Wild West. There are huge wheat farms and sprawling cattle ranches, big bustling cities, and oil. Alberta is where I first lived when I came to Canada and I love its bold ways and good-hearted people.

Cowboys still ride the range in Alberta. They have roundups and rodeos. In fact, the city of Calgary hosts one of the most famous rodeos, the Calgary Stampede. But real working cowboys are more likely to cross paths with oil derricks than the buffalo that once shared the land with them. A hundred years ago, when the settlers moved in, the buffalo were already on the edge of extinction. An effort has been made to bring the buffalo back, and today there is a large wild herd in Wood Buffalo National Park, a park that Alberta shares with the Northwest Territories.

Alberta has its own badlands, too. These dry lands with deep gullies and ravines got their name because it is so difficult for anything to grow or live there. But millions of years ago, dinosaurs walked here and the special nature of the Badlands has preserved their bones in layers of soil and sandstone. New and different species are still being unearthed, providing a rich, diverse record of the dinosaurs unmatched by any other fossil site. At the museum in Drumheller there are more complete dinosaur skeletons than anywhere else in the world.

BRITISH COLUMBIA

With its big cities and modern industry, British Columbia is like most places today. But I am always impressed by the mountains, the ocean, the wildlife, the trees—by the untouched beauty of this western province.

The Rocky Mountains are in its eastern part and the Coast Mountains that plunge right down into the Pacific Ocean are in the west. In between these two boundary chains are even more mountains. The people who live in the interior of the province have constructed their towns and villages in the long, narrow valleys between the towering peaks, because the mountains are too high and too steep to build on. The wildlife here has all but disappeared from the rest of North America: grizzly bears; cougars; gray wolves; eagles; and Pacific salmon.

Still, most British Columbians do not live in the mountains. They reside on the coast in the city of Vancouver, and on Vancouver Island and other small islands offshore. Here the climate is the mildest and rainiest in Canada. Its temperate rain forest extends farther north than any other like it in the world. A special park on Vancouver Island protects an ancient part of this rain forest. In it is a tree called the Carmanah Giant, said to be more than a thousand years old.

The islands and the coast have been inhabited for a very long time by a number of Native peoples who have rich, sophisticated cultures. These include the Haida, the Tlingit, the Kwakiutl, the Coast Salish, and the Bella Coola. Their ancestors created the first totem poles to record their mythologies and family histories. Some contemporary artists continue this tradition. These venerable carvings are symbols of Native peoples' pride in their heritage.

YUKON TERRITORY

The Yukon is the part of Canada I have chosen to call home. In a northern country, even Canadians consider it "the north." It has mountains and lakes, and there are the magical shimmering moments when the night sky comes alive with the glow of the Northern Lights. People come here to visit and some of them, like me, never leave.

The Yukon is the tundra. There are very few trees and the land is covered instead with low bushes, lichen, grass, and moss. In spite of its northerly location, much of the Yukon Territory escaped the total cover of the last Ice Age, so there are still plants growing here that were around when the great woolly mammoth roamed. Although the winters are cold, the summers are surprisingly warm. In the spring and summer, the ground is covered with the bright colors of the many wildflowers that grow here.

A gold rush in 1896 first focused the world's attention on the Yukon. Towns grew up almost overnight and hopeful gold hunters arrived by the hundreds. The gold rush passed and many of the towns became ghost towns. Poems and stories were written about that era, the land, and about the Mounties who kept the law. The legends began. They are still being told, and re-created, because there is something about this part of the world that makes a person want to do things that would seem impossible anywhere else.

NORTHWEST TERRITORIES

The Northwest Territories' huge area represents a third of all the land in Canada. It is nearly five times the size of Texas. Just 55,000 people live here, the same number of people that would fill a mid-sized town in southern Canada. It is a wonderland of vast open spaces filled with glacial lakes of every size and shape. This northern paradise gives me a complete sense of freedom and a feeling for the spaciousness and greatness of Canada.

Here a wolf trails a barren-ground caribou. Figures of stone, called "inukshuk," are used by the Inuit, a Native people, to mark their trails so they will not get lost. The inukshuks stand out even in the winter because it is so cold that the snow is too powdery and light to settle on the figures. It can get as low as –64° F, and in some areas, there are as few as thirty frost-free days a year.

History is being made in the Northwest Territories today. The people of the territories have voted to divide it into two regions. One of them, Nunavut, will be five times the size of California. With a population that is eighty percent Inuit, it is the result of the largest Native land claim in Canadian history.

O CANADA

English text by R. STANLEY WEIR, D.C.L.
Paroles françaises de L'Hon. Judge ROUTHIER

Musique de CALIXA LAVALLÉE
Harmonisé par R. Stanley Weir

1. O   Can - a - da!   Our home and na - tive   land! ____
1. Ô   Can - a - da!   Ter - re de nos aï - eux, ____

True   pa - triot love   in   all thy sons com - mand.
Ton   front est ceint   de   fleu-rons glo - ri - eux!

With glow-ing hearts we_ see thee rise The_True North strong and free;
Car ton bras sait por - ter l'é - pé - e Il sait por - ter la croix!

From far and wide O_ Can - a - da, We   stand on guard for   thee.
Ton his-toire est une é - po - pé - e Des   plus bril-lants ex - ploits.